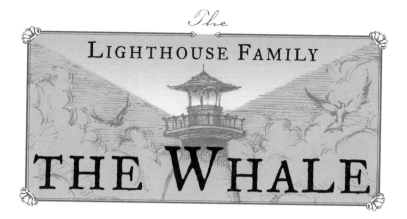

The

LIGHTHOUSE FAMILY

THE WHALE

The
LIGHTHOUSE FAMILY

THE WHALE

BY CYNTHIA RYLANT
ILLUSTRATED BY PRESTON McDANIELS

SIMON & SCHUSTER BOOKS FOR YOUNG READERS
New York   London   Toronto   Sydney   Singapore

For D. P. and the little dog in his boat —C. R.
With love for my wife —P. McD.

SIMON & SCHUSTER BOOKS FOR YOUNG READERS
An imprint of Simon & Schuster Children's Publishing Division
1230 Avenue of the Americas, New York, New York 10020

The text for this book is set in Centaur.
The illustrations for this book are rendered in graphite.
Manufactured in the United States of America

2 4 6 8 10 9 7 5 3 1

CIP Data for this book is available from the Library of Congress.
ISBN 0-689-84881-1

first edition

CONTENTS

1. *The Family* 6

2. *The Whale* 16

3. *Some Help* 24

4. *Some Company* 34

5. *The Mother* 42

6. *A Friend Forever* 54

1. The Family

In a lonely lighthouse there lived a family of animals who were, in fact, not lonely at all.

Their lighthouse stood on top of a cliff of sharp rocks beside the sea. And it looked as if it were the most forlorn and empty place in the world, standing there all alone.

But if one drew closer to this lighthouse, everything about it changed.

For there were blue petunias growing in window boxes at the little cottage next door.

In the yard sunflowers lined a lovely picket fence and tomatoes and carrots grew in the garden.

At the base of the lighthouse was a handmade wooden wagon filled with toys, and the toys themselves were handmade: penguins that wobbled, pelicans with large beaks that opened and closed, crabs with movable, clicking legs.

If one drew even closer to the front door of the keeper's cottage, the smell of fresh-baked bread or berry dumplings floated out onto the wind.

And, looking inside this open door, there one would find the happiest family in the world.

They were: Pandora, the cat; Seabold, the dog; and three mouse children—Whistler, Lila, and their baby sister, Tiny.

They had lived here together for less than a year. But already they had made it a home.

On this particular summer day, Whistler and Lila were preparing for a shell-gathering trip along the beach. Whistler had a project.

"We are going to collect broken clamshells," he told Pandora, the cat, as she refilled his cup with warm ginger tea. "And then I am going to build a birdhouse and decorate it with the shells and put it on a post in the garden."

"Lovely!" Pandora purred. "It will have the

feeling of the sea and the birds will be happy."

"It was my idea," said Whistler's sister Lila.

"It's true," said Whistler. "Lila thought of it. I'm simply carrying it out."

"Wonderful," Pandora said.

"But I'll help collect the shells," said Lila. "Then I have to finish sewing an apron for my doll."

Lila held up a small wooden mouse doll. It had a tiny blue bonnet, large painted eyes, and a simple flowered dress. It looked a bit like Lila herself.

"I do love summertime, don't you?" Pandora purred happily, slicing another piece of brown bread for Whistler.

"Oh yes," said Lila. Whistler nodded vigorously.

"And," said Lila, "I love summertime better here than any other place in the world."

Hearing this warmed Pandora's heart. Some days she could not quite believe she had been blessed with this little family. For she had first lived all alone at the lighthouse. For four long years she had baked bread for none but herself, poured tea for no one

else, and kept the great lamp shining without the help of another.

But all that changed when a dog named Seabold and his broken boat washed ashore one day. For Seabold stayed on with Pandora while his injured leg mended, through fall, then winter, then into spring. As he repaired his beloved boat, Seabold thought surely he would return to the ocean and again sail the wide world.

But then one day they found the children— orphans—floating in a crate and lost, and Pandora and Seabold took them in. They tended to these little ones, cared and cooked for them, tucked them in each evening and welcomed them awake in morning.

And, of course, in time, something very important changed: their hearts. For the three mouse children made of this cottage and its solitary lighthouse a real home. With stories to tell. Bread to bake. Flowers to grow. Games to play.

And Seabold, who had thought he would always

live a solitary life, could not leave. For he was a family dog now, and he was needed.

As Whistler and Lila finished their bread and tea this summer morning, Seabold took Tiny to the lagoon to look at the giant sun starfish. These were quite amazing creatures, for they were enormous and had twenty—Seabold counted—twenty legs! They rested in the shallow water or on the cold wet rocks and thought their starfish thoughts. Tiny watched them from the roll of Seabold's soft cap,

where she loved to ride, and gurgled happily.

Seabold smiled. He was quite attached to Tiny.

On their way back to the cottage, they passed Whistler and Lila heading for the shore with twine bags in their small paws.

"Lovely morning, children!" said Seabold. "And how are you this day?"

The brother and sister told him of their plans.

"Splendid!" said Seabold. "I must clean the lanterns in the lighthouse or I'd join you myself. But have a wonderful time," he added. "And keep a sharp eye for adventures!"

Seabold always said this to the children as they went off anywhere. It was no wonder that he chose the name *Adventure* for his dear boat.

Still, most days at the lighthouse were simple, quiet sea days, with happy times but no real adventures.

This day, though, would be a lucky one.

This day would have an adventure.

2. The Whale

Whistler and Lila were walking along the rocky shore, happily collecting shells, when from out in the water came a long, sad cry.

"What's that?" asked Lila, stopping and looking across the sea.

She and Whistler stood very still and listened.

There it was again. The saddest, loneliest cry they had ever heard.

Whistler scrambled up a tall stick. Lila followed.

"Who's there?" called Whistler as loudly as he could (and a small mouse voice is not very loud).

"Who's there?" Lila called after him.

Most fortunately, most luckily, most wonderful for all, the creature who was crying had *very* good ears.

Up from the water popped a shiny white head.

"*Me!*" the creature called, and began to cry.

"My goodness!" said Lila. "It's a baby whale!"

And indeed it was. A baby beluga whale, in fact. And, oh, how it could cry.

"We'll be right there!" shouted Whistler. "Don't move!"

And within minutes the two children had run for their small boat (built for them by Seabold) and were rowing out to the whale.

When they finally reached him, the baby beluga was quite exhausted. Too exhausted even to cry anymore. He simply looked at them with frantic, frightened eyes.

"I've lost my mother," he whimpered.

"Oh, dear!" said Lila in distress. Being an orphan, Lila was very sensitive to babies with lost mothers.

"Where did you lose her?" asked Whistler.

The beluga looked as if he might start crying again. But he didn't.

"Somewhere," he said. "We were swimming and a big pod of humpbacks came through, and there were so many, and I saw a baby I thought I could play with and I followed him and then . . . and then . . ."

The baby whale sobbed.

"Then the humpbacks swam away all of a sudden and I was by myself."

"Oh, *dear*," said Lila.

The little whale floated silently. He was looking most tragic. The two mouse children gazed at him with deepest sympathy.

Suddenly Whistler declared, "*We* will find your mother!"

Lila looked at him in surprise.

The beluga's eyes brightened.

"Really?" he said. "You can find her?"

"Definitely. We are experts at finding lost mothers," Whistler fibbed.

Lila looked at him in even greater surprise.

"Here's what I want you to do," Whistler said to

the baby. "Oh, by the way—what is your name?"

"Sebastian," said the whale. Whistler introduced himself and Lila.

"Very happy to meet you," said the well-mannered, tear-soaked beluga.

Whistler resumed. "Here's what I want you to do," he said. "Do you see that lagoon over there?"

The baby nodded his head.

"I want you to go over there and rest," said Whistler. "It's quite nice, the water is warm, and sometimes an otter comes along with a good story."

The whale nodded again.

"All right," he said.

"What is your mother's name?" Whistler asked.

"Mama," said the whale.

"No, no," said Lila. "He means her *real* name."

"Oh," said the baby. "Everybody calls her Honey."

"Honey?" repeated Lila. "What a nice name."

"She's a nice mama," said the beluga.

"Now you go over to the lagoon and wait for us, all right?" said Whistler.

"All right," answered Sebastian. "I'm a little sleepy anyway."

"Of course you are," said Lila.

"See you soon," said Whistler. "Don't worry."

As they watched the baby beluga swim toward the lagoon, Lila whispered to Whistler, "And just how are we going to find that mama whale?"

Whistler whispered back, "I have *no* idea."

Then he looked squarely at Lila.

"But we are going to *do* it!"

3. Some Help

Of course, the first thing Lila and Whistler did was to find Pandora. Seabold was very good at making toys and fixing boats. But it was Pandora who could always figure things out.

And after she heard the children's story as they all stood together in the vegetable garden, Pandora took a few moments to think.

Then she said, "I have an idea."

The children knew she would.

Now, though Pandora had lived many years all by herself at the lighthouse, she had, in that time, made some acquaintances.

They were creatures very different from her, creatures always on the move, but she had learned a few names and had, from time to time, even called on these ocean neighbors for help.

And one neighbor she had relied on before was a cranky old bird—a cormorant named Huck.

Huck didn't like anybody. He kept to himself and spent most of his time on top of a piling on the south side of the island, airing out his wings. He was a soggy old bird, and he loved nothing better than to spread out his wings and stand for hours feeling the breeze.

But even though Huck liked no one, he would *help anyone.*

And once, when Pandora had fallen into a large bramble bush and was all caught up in thorns, Huck— who just happened to be flying by—stopped and helped her pick her way out. He grumbled the whole time about what a "mucky muddle" and a "sticky stickle" she'd gotten herself into.

But he did help her and seemed pleased to do it.

Afterward, Huck told Pandora if she ever needed him again, to flash the great lamp five times—quickly—in the direction of the old piling he stood on. And he'd be by.

Since that time Pandora had called on him only once more, to ask directions to a cherry orchard she'd heard about but didn't know how to find. She had needed to make a medicinal tea for a sick puffin passing through. But she was careful not to bother Huck unnecessarily. She knew he was crotchety.

This day, though, Huck was her best idea. Huck would help find the mother whale.

Pandora found Seabold, who had laid Tiny down for a nap, and explained the situation.

"I'll go flash the lamp," Seabold said. "You stay in the yard and watch for Huck."

Seabold climbed the four steep flights of stairs and then the ladder into the lantern room. He lit all

the wicks and turned the great lamp southeast. Then he flashed the light five quick times.

Within minutes Huck was landing in the yard where Pandora and the children stood waiting.

"Criminy," Huck complained. "That's some wind today."

He shook out his feathers and cleared his throat and coughed up a bit of . . . *something*. No one could be sure what.

Lila and Whistler looked at each other with wide eyes.

But Pandora merely smiled kindly at the cormorant.

"Thank you for coming, Huck," she said. "We have a problem and we need your help."

"Well, don't dillydally," grumbled Huck.

And Pandora explained. When she concluded her story she asked, "Huck, do you think you might fly over the sea and look for this missing mother? You will be able to travel so fast and so far."

"And," Pandora added wisely, "you know the waters better than anyone."

Huck was still frowning, but she could see in his eyes that he was pleased. Underneath all the growling, Huck really just wanted to be appreciated.

He gave a quick nod of his head.

"I can do that," he said. "What's her name?"

"Honey," Whistler and Lila said together.

"And you say she's a beluga?" he asked.

The children nodded their heads.

"That helps," said Huck, "her being all white. She'll shine like a light."

Then Whistler cleared his throat and stepped forward.

"Mr. Huck," he said with a serious face, "may we go with you, Lila and me?"

Lila's mouth dropped open in surprise. As did Pandora's.

Huck set off into a great deal of coughing and hacking and spitting. Finally he looked squarely at Whistler.

"Well, I don't see why not," he said.

Then he looked toward Pandora.

"As long as it's all right with you, Pandora," he added. "I figure three sets of eyes will get the job done faster."

Pandora looked at Whistler and Lila with a bit of worry on her face.

"If you go with Huck, you must hold on tight," she said.

The children promised they would.

"And you must be home before nightfall," said Pandora.

The children promised again.

Pandora smiled. She had every confidence in them.

And soon, Lila and Whistler were riding the back of a cormorant, out across the wide blue sea.

4. Some Company

When Huck and the children had disappeared into the faraway sky, Pandora turned back toward the lighthouse and climbed the stairs to find Seabold in the tower.

The dog's face was pressed close to the window.

"Did I just see Whistler and Lila fly by?" he asked.

"You did," said Pandora. "They are going to help Huck find the mother."

Seabold smiled.

"What an adventure for two children," he said. Seabold truly loved adventure.

"I told Huck he must have them home by nightfall," said Pandora.

"Of course," answered Seabold. "And what of the baby?" he asked.

"She's asleep in the cottage," said Pandora.

"No, no," said Seabold. "The *other* baby."

"Oh," Pandora smiled. "The other baby is still resting in the lagoon, waiting for his mother."

"Hmmm," said Seabold. "I expect he must be feeling a little lonely."

"Yes," said Pandora.

"And a little afraid," added Seabold.

"Yes."

"I think I shall go keep him company," said Seabold, starting for the stairs.

"What did you say his name was?" he called halfway down.

"Sebastian!" answered Pandora. She listened as Seabold descended to the bottom and went out the door. And she smiled in deep satisfaction, to have a friend so kind.

Pandora then returned to the cottage to make a stew and to watch over Tiny.

When Seabold reached the lagoon, the baby whale was swimming in circles.

"Hello, Sebastian!" called Seabold.

The whale stopped and put his head out of the water to look.

"Hello," he answered in a small sad voice. "Who are you?"

The dog smiled and saluted.

"I am Seabold," he said. "Once a sailor of the sea, now the keeper of a lighthouse and three small mice."

"Lila and Whistler!" said Sebastian, perking up.

"And their baby sister, Tiny," said Seabold. "And, indeed, Lila and Whistler are off to find your mother."

"Oh, good," said Sebastian. "For I miss her so much."

The small whale looked as if he might cry at any moment. Seabold could see that he must do something.

"Do you like tricks?" he asked the whale.

Sebastian brightened.

"Yes!" he said.

"I have a trick," said Seabold, and he stood on his head.

The little whale thumped his tail on the water with delight.

"That was very good!" he told Seabold.

"And do *you* have a trick?" asked the dog.

The whale thought a moment.

"Yes!" he said. And he dove under the water. He was gone several moments, and just as Seabold was beginning to worry and to think of diving in, the baby surfaced. He gave a big full spray of water from his spout and there, on top, bounced a very surprised crab.

"Hey!" said the crab.

Sebastian stopped spraying, and the crab, mumbling and griping, swam back under.

Seabold laughed and clapped his paws.

"That was a good one!" he said.

Sebastian smiled shyly. He liked this dog Seabold.

"And now," said Seabold, drawing nearer the edge of the water to settle upon a rock, "would you like to hear a story?"

"A story?" asked Sebastian. "Oh yes!" He swam very near.

"Then I shall tell you a wonderful story," said Seabold.

He leaned forward.

"Once upon a time there was a brave baby beluga named Sebastian. . . ."

The little whale's eyes shone and a smile spread across his face.

He grew very quiet and listened.

5. The Mother

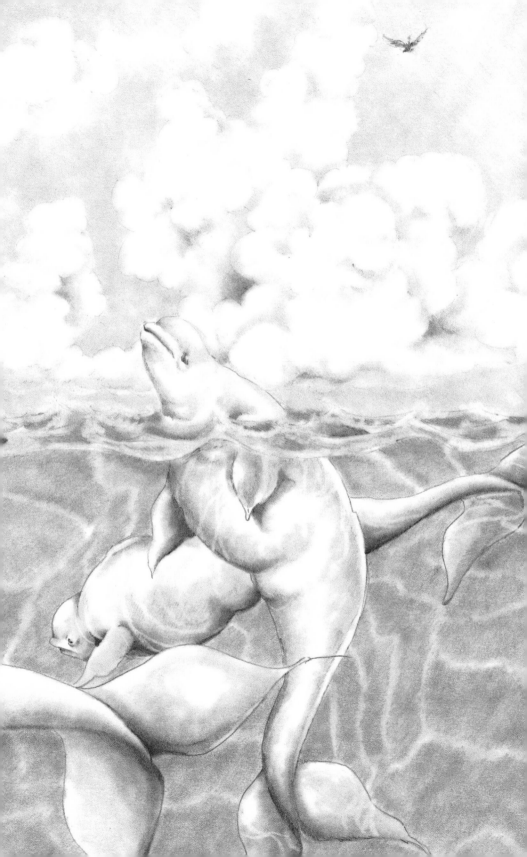

While Seabold was telling Sebastian all about the brave baby beluga, two other children were also being very brave. And also not having much luck.

Whistler and Lila, holding tight to Huck's back, were searching and searching the sea. And this was not easy. The ocean is vast, and even a whale will be but a speck in its waters. And if you are searching through tiny mouse eyes from the back of an old cormorant, your job will be especially hard.

"Oh, dear," said Lila after they had searched for what seemed several hours, "how will we ever find her?"

Whistler peered down toward the miles and miles of open sea.

"We will," he said.

"But what if we *don't?*" asked Lila.

"We *will*," said Whistler.

"What's all that yacking back there?" yelled Huck. It was so windy Huck could barely hear the small voices on his back.

"Lila says she's *sure* we will find the mother!" yelled Whistler, grinning at his sister. Lila could not help grinning back.

"*Who's* got a brother?" yelled Huck.

Whistler just laughed and shook his head.

And they all kept searching.

Another hour passed. And another. And yet another.

And as long as the two children and the old bird stayed in the air longer and longer, the cormorant's age began to show. His flapping slowed. His flying wobbled. And sometimes he lost altitude and Lila was sure they were about to crash.

"Are you okay?" Whistler would yell.

"Did *what* today?" Huck would yell back.

Whistler and Lila exchanged worried looks and

held tighter to the old bird's back. The day was growing darker. They had to be home by night. And there still was no mother, and now with Huck wheezing and wobbling and . . .

"Look!" yelled Lila.

"Where?" asked Whistler.

"Out there," Lila pointed. *"Way out there,"* she said firmly.

"I don't see anything," said Whistler.

"I do," said Lila. She crawled closer to Huck's ear.

"Turn left, Huck," she shouted. "Left toward the horizon!"

"You don't have to yell," complained the bird. "I can hear just fine."

He turned left and flew.

"Keep going, keep going," said Lila. "They're out there."

"Who?" asked Whistler, trying hard to see what Lila saw.

"The whole pod," said Lila. "The *whole pod* of belugas!"

And sure enough, as Huck covered the water, all three began to see a marvelous pod of white whales swimming and spouting up ahead.

"Hooray!" shouted Whistler.

When they were finally above the whales, Whistler called to one.

"May we land?" he called.

"Excuse me?" the whale replied.

"May we land on your back?" Whistler called.

"Pardon me?" said the whale.

"Oh, *posh*," said Huck, and he simply did it. He landed on the whale's back.

"Hey!" said the whale.

"Don't worry," said Whistler, climbing off Huck's back and onto the whale's. "We're just look-ing for a beluga named Honey. We found her baby."

"You found Honey's baby?" cried the whale. "Oh, joy!"

"Marilyn!" the beluga called to the whale in front of him. "They've found Honey's baby!"

"Honey's baby?" said Marilyn.

"Freddie!" she called to the beluga in front of her. "They've found Honey's baby!"

And so the calling went, through the pod, one whale to the next, until Honey—Sebastian's poor, frantic, unhappy mama—was found.

She swam to the mouse children.

"We've been searching everywhere!" Honey told Whistler and Lila. *"Everywhere!"*

Her eyes filled up with tears.

"Is my baby all right?" she asked.

"He's great!" said Whistler. "He's at our house!"

"Your *house*?" asked Honey.

"You'll see," said Whistler. "Just follow us. Hurry!"

He climbed back up on Huck.

"Let's go, Huck!" said Whistler.

"Let's go!" said Lila, climbing up.

And Huck tried to go. He wanted to go. He flapped his feeble wings and worked to go.

But he just couldn't.

"I'm all out of gas, kids," Huck said with a tired

old wheeze. "These old bones just aren't going to make it."

He gave a heavy sigh.

"You go on and ride back with Honey. I'll stay out here tonight and rest up."

"Go back without you?" cried Lila.

"Never!" said Whistler.

"You're the *hero*, Huck," said Lila, patting his old head. "You have to come back with us. In fact, we won't leave without you."

Huck frowned. (Though deep down he was happy.)

"I will gladly give *all* of you a ride," said Honey.

Huck continued to frown.

"*Please*, Huck," said Lila.

"Sir," said Honey, "I am very anxious to see my

baby, so I must ask you, *please.* You have done your noble duty."

Huck liked that word—*noble*—very much.

"All right, all right," he grumbled, settling down on Honey's back. "I just hope no pelicans see me."

"We'll tell them you're a hero, Huck," said Whistler.

"*Our* hero," added Lila.

Huck coughed and hacked and tried his very best not to smile.

But he did anyway. Just a little.

Then they all journeyed home on the back of a whale.

6. A Friend Forever

Pandora was wise enough to keep the lamp burning in the lighthouse, just in case Huck and the children were unable to keep their promise to be home before dark. And indeed it was the light that helped Honey find her way to the correct shore and to the lagoon where her little one waited.

When the mother whale swam nearer the lagoon, she and her passengers saw a wonderful sight. Pandora and Seabold were sitting on top of a rock—Tiny perched in Seabold's cap—and they were feeding the baby whale big spoonfuls of vegetable stew.

"Sebastian!" called the mother beluga.

The little whale's head turned.

"Mama!" he cried, bits of carrot falling from his mouth.

Oh, it was a joyous reunion. Huck flew off the whale's back and deposited the mice children safely on shore, where they were hugged tight again and again. And the happy beluga mother and son swam around and around, nudging heads close, nestling their bodies together, clicking and singing and laughing.

When all the hellos were over and the time had finally come for good-byes, Whistler asked baby

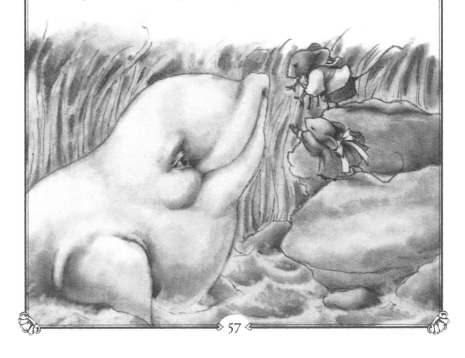

Sebastian, "Will you ever come back to see us?"

"I will always come back to see you," answered Sebastian. "I am your friend forever."

And with that, and their deepest thanks, mother whale and baby swam off to join their pod.

It was night now, and suddenly the mouse children felt so very weary.

"Pandora, is there any more stew?" asked Whistler.

"Plenty more," answered Pandora. "Plenty for everyone. Including you, our good friend, Huck."

The old bird coughed and shook his feathers.

"No need to bother," he said.

"It's no bother, Huck," said Seabold. "Why, a bowl of stew is the least we can do for your noble effort today."

There was that word again, that word that Huck liked so much: noble.

"Please come with us, Huck," said Lila, taking the old bird's wing.

So they all walked back to the cottage, where

Pandora and Seabold ladled out big thick bowls of stew and watched with pleasure as the old bird and the children ate and ate and ate.

After supper, Huck was given Seabold's favorite chair, to rest his wings before going home.

But the old cormorant fell asleep and would not wake until morning.

The three mouse children, lovingly tucked into their warm sock-bed by the fire, were also asleep

before Pandora could even kiss them good night.

And out in the vast dark waters of the ocean, a mother and a baby were a family again. Soon they would join their larger family, amid those happy calls with which lost ones are always welcomed home.

For everyone, it had been *quite* an adventurous day.